CARTOON NETWORK®

SCOOBY-DOO!™ AND THE

FARMYARD FRIGHT

Look for the **Scooby-Doo Mysteries.**
Collect them all!

Written by
James Gelsey

A
LITTLE APPLE
PAPERBACK

SCHOLASTIC INC.
New York Toronto London Auckland Sydney
Mexico City New Delhi Hong Kong

ISBN 0-439-18881-4

Designed by Carisa Swenson

12 11 10 9 8 7 6 5 4 3 2 1   1 2 3 4 5 6/0

Special thanks to Duendes del Sur for cover and interior illustrations.
Printed in the U.S.A.
First Scholastic printing, July 2001

For Vanessa

" **F** red, are you sure we're not lost?" Shaggy asked from the back of the Mystery Machine. "It feels like we've been driving for days."

"Shaggy, it's only been forty-five minutes," Velma answered.

"Yeah? My stomach thinks it's been forty-five hours," Shaggy replied. "When can we stop for a snack?"

"We're not stopping until we get to Dalrymple's Farm," Fred said.

"You dragged me and Scooby-Doo hundreds of miles away from civilization to go to a farm?" asked Shaggy. "We don't like farms. They're so boring."

"Reah, roring," Scooby echoed.

"I think you'll like this one," Daphne said. "They have a barnyard petting area."

"And hayrides," Fred added.

Shaggy and Scooby looked at each other and made enormous pretend yawns.

"And a big farmhouse barbecue," Velma said.

Scooby's ears perked up. "Rarecue?" he asked.

"Why didn't you say so?" Shaggy said. "Scooby and I love farms."

Daphne looked out the window of the van. There was a huge billboard by the side of the road.

"'Future site of Shepard Farms luxury houses,'" she read. "Gosh, it's so sad how all these farms are being gobbled up by real-estate developers.'"

"Pretty soon, there won't be any farms left," agreed Velma.

Just past the billboard, the gang noticed a small homemade sign at the side of the road.

"'Turn here for the Great Dalrymple Corn Maze,'" Daphne read.

"The great who what?" asked Shaggy.

"Corn maze," Velma said matter-of-factly. "It's a giant maze cut into a cornfield. It's the only one like it around."

"It's officially opening tomorrow, but we're getting a sneak preview today," Daphne said. "I'm doing a story on it for the school paper, remember?"

Fred steered the Mystery Machine down a long dirt road. Rows and rows of cornstalks grew along both sides. Suddenly, a scarecrow ran out of the cornfield and into the middle of the road. Fred slammed on the brakes.

"Zoinks!" Shaggy exclaimed. "It's a runaway scarecrow!"

The scarecrow ran over to the van and held up a big sign to the windshield.

"'Leave or pay the price'!" Fred read.

"What do you think that means?" Daphne asked.

"I think it means we're supposed to buy an admission ticket," Velma suggested.

"Or that Mr. Creepy Scarecrow wants us to leave!" Shaggy said. "So let's turn this van around and head back to town."

The scarecrow roared at the gang. Then he turned and ran back into the cornfield.

"That was odd," Velma said.

"Daphne, make sure you ask Mr. Dalrymple about that scarecrow when you interview him," Fred said.

"I've already added it to my list of questions," Daphne said, showing him her notebook.

Soon they pulled up in front of a big red farmhouse.

A large animal pen with sheep, goats, and

other animals stood off to one side. Large haystacks dotted the open land around the farmhouse. A few other cars were parked out front.

"Here we are, gang," Fred said. "Everybody out."

As soon as the gang filed out of the van, Scooby felt a tickle in his nose.

"Ra-ra-ra-CHOOOOO!" he sneezed.

"Gesundheit, Scooby," Velma replied.

"What's the matter, pal?" asked Shaggy. "Allergies?"

"Ray rever." Scooby nodded. "Ra-CHOOO!"

"Poor Scooby," Daphne said. "We'll stay just long enough for me to talk to Mr. Dalrymple. Then we'll go back home."

"No, hold on a minute," Shaggy said. "We didn't come all this way just to turn around and leave. Not with a big farmhouse barbecue coming up."

"Is that all right with you, Scooby?" asked Velma.

"Rou ret-CHOOO!" Scooby barked.

"That's my pal," Shaggy said. "Thinking with his stomach instead of his nose!"

Chapter 2

The gang walked over to a group of people gathered on the farmhouse porch.

"Excuse us," Fred said. "We're looking for Mr. Dalrymple."

A man wearing denim overalls, a yellow work shirt, and a big straw hat turned around and smiled.

"That's me!" he announced. "Who wants to know?"

"I do, Mr. Dalrymple," Daphne said. "I'm Daphne Blake. I spoke to you about an interview for my school paper."

"Of course, Daphne," he replied with a smile. "But please, call me Farmer Joe."

"Nice to meet you, Farmer Joe," Daphne replied. "These are my friends. This is Fred, Velma, Shaggy, and Scooby-Doo."

"Welcome to Dalrymple's Farm, home of the Great Dalrymple Corn Maze," he said with a big grin. "Now I have to finish up with these other reporters first. Why don't you all take a little look around?"

"Groovy," Daphne said.

"By the way, Farmer Joe, I liked that scarecrow who greets the visitors," Velma said. "But some people may find him a little creepy."

"Find who a little creepy?" asked Farmer Joe.

"You know, the person you hired to dress up like a scarecrow and run out into the road to remind guests they'll have to pay to get in," Fred said.

"I didn't hire anybody to dress as a scarecrow," Farmer Joe replied. "Are you kids sure?"

"Uh, we must've made a mistake," Velma said quickly. "What do you say we have that look around now?"

"The petting area is on the far side of the farmhouse," Farmer Joe said with a smile. "The maze and hayride are out back, but I'd rather you let me take you out to the maze myself. Oh, and the barbecue's going to be on the back porch."

"Like, that's all I needed to know," Shaggy said. "Come on, Scooby, let's go so we'll be first in line."

"Not so fast, you two," Velma said. "We're going around back with you."

"Why?" Shaggy asked. "It's not like anything

can happen to us between here and there."

"We just want to make sure," Fred said, grinning.

As the gang walked around the farmhouse, they passed a tall pile of huge burlap bags.

"Man, those are the biggest tea bags I've ever seen," Shaggy said.

"Those aren't tea bags, Shaggy," Velma explained. "Farmer Joe uses those bags to hold the corn after it's picked."

They looked up and saw a woman walking toward them backward. She was measuring the side of the house. She was trying very hard to keep the far end of the tape from moving as she unrolled the tape measure in her hand. Just as she reached the gang, Scooby let out a gigantic sneeze.

"Ra-ra-ra-CHOOOOOO!"

The woman jumped and dropped the measuring tape. The long yellow strip zipped along the ground and snapped back into the case.

"Rorry," Scooby apologized.

"Oh, that's all right," the woman said quickly. "I think I got the measurement anyway."

"Is that so, Sally Ann?" asked Farmer Joe. He had come around the side of the house just after Scooby sneezed. "Since I won't sell you my land, are you trying to figure out a way to take my house?"

"Just gathering some measurements for our models," the woman replied, wiping her dusty hands on a red bandanna in her pocket. "We want the houses of Shepard Farms to look authentic."

"Shepard Farms? Didn't we see that name on a billboard?" Velma asked.

"Right next door," Farmer Joe said with a nod. "Sally Ann's company just bought the Shepard farm next door. And now Sally Ann wants me to sell, too."

"We paid the Shepards top dollar for their land. More than they'd ever be able to make farming it," Sally Ann said. "And we're willing to pay you a whole lot more than that silly maze of yours will ever bring in."

"Now, see here, Sally Ann," Farmer Joe said. "The Great Dalrymple Corn Maze is just the thing to bring in enough visitors to keep my farm going."

"And it's also just the thing to bring in traffic jams, tour buses, and other things that will upset the people who will be moving into the Shepard Farms development," Sally

Ann retorted. "Mark my words, Joe Dalrymple, when I'm through with you, the Great Dalrymple Corn Maze will be nothing more than a memory."

Sally Ann snatched her measuring tape from the ground and walked away. As she turned the corner, the gang heard her shriek. Then a sheep wandered around the side of the house.

"Matilda!" Farmer Joe called. "How'd you get out of the petting area?"

The sound of a man's voice yelling, "Help!" suddenly echoed through the air.

"That sounds like Dusty!" exclaimed Farmer Joe. "One of you kids grab Matilda, and the rest of you follow me!"

Chapter 3

Farmer Joe, Fred, Velma, and Daphne ran off to see what had happened, leaving Shaggy and Scooby behind to catch the sheep. It was minding its own business, quietly grazing on a patch of grass.

"Okay, Scooby-Doo, you're a dog," Shaggy said. "Go catch the sheep."

"Ruh-ruh," Scooby said, shaking his head. "Ri'm rot a reepdog."

"I know that, Scoob, but the sheep doesn't. Maybe you could pretend," Shaggy suggested.

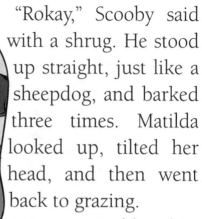

"Rokay," Scooby said with a shrug. He stood up straight, just like a sheepdog, and barked three times. Matilda looked up, tilted her head, and then went back to grazing.

"No, try it like this, Scoob," Shaggy said. He got down on all fours and started barking like a dog. The sheep didn't even look up this time.

"I guess I'm not much of a sheepdog, either," Shaggy said.

Scooby felt another tickle in his nose and let out a big sneeze.

"Ra-ra-ra-ra-CHOOOO!"

The startled sheep let out a loud bleat and ran toward the cornfield.

"Quick, Scooby, head it off at the pass,"

Shaggy called. "We don't want it to get lost in the cornfield."

Scooby took off after the sheep, but it was too late. It had disappeared into the cornfield. A moment later, they heard a rustling sound coming from the cornstalks.

"Psst, Scooby," whispered Shaggy. "I think it's over there." They walked a few steps. Shaggy reached over and pushed the cornstalks aside.

"Rikes!" Scooby shouted, jumping into Shaggy's arms. He threw his arms around Shaggy's head.

A tall man with a goatee and a red bandanna around his neck walked out of the cornfield.

"Oh, I am so sorry," he said. "I did not mean to scare your dog. I was just going for a walk in the field. For inspiration."

"Like, what kind of inspiration can you get from cornstalks?" asked Shaggy, trying to pry Scooby off his head.

"Artistic. I am Fortunato, and I create living art," the man said. "Not unlike the Great Fortunato Corn Maze."

"Don't you mean the Great Dalrymple Corn Maze?" asked Shaggy.

"Why should it be called the Great Dalrymple Corn Maze when I, the Great Fortunato, created it?" asked Fortunato.

"I give up," said Shaggy. "Why should it?"

"It shouldn't!" Fortunato shot back. "I came here from the city to find inspiration in nature. Farmer Joe let me wander his farmland. To thank him, I gave him one of my drawings. Like this."

Fortunato took a folded piece of paper from his pocket and showed it to Shaggy. It was a drawing of a maze.

"Like, is this the maze that everyone's talking about?" asked Shaggy.

"As a matter of fact, it is," Fortunato continued. "I never said Farmer Joe could turn my art into a giant corn maze. Now he's going to charge admission and take all the credit. This is not right. No one steals from Fortunato and gets away with it!"

"Ra-ra-ra-CHOOO!" Scooby sneezed so hard he fell and sprawled onto the ground.

"Well, it was, uh, nice meeting you, Mr.

Fortunato," Shaggy said, helping Scooby up. "Come on, Scoob. We'd better go tell Farmer Joe we lost his sheep."

"When you see him, tell him he hasn't heard the last of Fortunato!" yelled the angry artist as he wandered back into the cornfield.

"If you ask me, Scoob, that guy is a few kernels short of a corncob," Shaggy said. "Let's get out of here before he comes back."

Chapter 4

Shaggy and Scooby walked around the farmhouse to the petting area. They saw the rest of the gang and Farmer Joe talking to another man.

"Are you sure, Dusty?" asked Farmer Joe.

"I tell ya, I saw him with my own eyes when I came out of the house!" the man exclaimed. "The scarecrow opened the gate and chased all the animals out. Then he ran off into the cornfield. I managed to get all the animals back except for Matilda."

"Speaking of Matilda, where is she?"

Farmer Joe asked Shaggy and Scooby.

"She, like, went for a walk . . . in the cornfield," Shaggy admitted.

"Rorry," Scooby barked.

"Scooby and I tried to catch her, but she was too fast," Shaggy explained. "Then some weird guy named Fortunato came out of the field and scared Scooby."

"He's the fellow I was telling you about, the one who gave me the drawing of the maze," Farmer Joe said. "Once I finished making it, he started pestering me about giving him credit and half of the money it makes. A real crazy artist, that one. Well, enough jabbering, I'd better go find Matilda." Farmer Joe walked off into the cornfield to look for his lost sheep. "I tell ya, that scarecrow was the strangest thing I ever saw," Dusty continued, wiping his forehead with a red bandanna. "I've been on this farm going on thirty years now. And I've never seen a scarecrow come to life before. Then again, I'm getting used to seeing a lot of things I've never seen before."

"Like what?" asked Daphne.

"Like a maze cut into a cornfield," Dusty said angrily. "Stupidest thing I ever heard. Now we'll have all kinds of rude city folk trampling everywhere, upsetting the animals. It's like I told Farmer Joe a thousand times . . ."

"This is a farm, not an amusement park," Farmer Joe recited as he walked over with Matilda. He unlocked the gate and nudged Matilda inside the pen. Then he locked the gate and walked over to the gang. "Dusty here is worried for the animals."

"Someone's got to be," Dusty interrupted. "I'm out here every day with the chickens and cows and sheep and horses and goats and all the others. Did you ever consider how upsetting this maze is going to be to them? Then there's that scarecrow fellow frightening guests as they drive up, and spooking the animals. Who knows what else he'll do?"

"Dusty, how about you make sure the animals are okay and then finish your chores?" Farmer Joe suggested. "I'm going to show these kids the maze."

"Groovy," Daphne said. "I can't wait to see it."

Farmer Joe led them to the back of the farmhouse. He opened a small metal box mounted on the red siding and took out a microphone. He flipped a switch and started to speak.

"Attention, guests, please join us at the maze entrance," he announced. His voice echoed through loudspeakers all over the farm. As he put the microphone back, he added, "I put this in so folks in the maze could hear my announcements. You know, in case they lose track of time or something."

Farmer Joe then led the gang to the edge of the cornfield. A scarecrow holding a sign that read THIS WAY stood next to a path.

"Ruh-roh," Scooby said as he hid behind Shaggy.

"Don't be afraid, Scooby," Farmer Joe said. "This scarecrow isn't real. None of 'em are."

"You mean there are more?" whimpered Shaggy.

"Sure, I've got scarecrows like this one all over the place," Farmer Joe continued. "They've got signs telling people which way they can go and such."

The gang followed Farmer Joe down the short path to a small clearing in the cornfield. A giant GREAT DALRYMPLE CORN MAZE banner stood over the break in a row of cornstalks. Some reporters were already there, taking pictures.

"Well, here we are," Farmer Joe proudly announced.

"Like, I don't see a maze," Shaggy said. "All I see is more cornstalks."

"That's the maze, Shaggy," Velma said. "If you wanted to see the whole thing, you'd have to look down at it from a hundred feet in the air."

"Hey, Farmer Joe, I've got a question!" called one of the reporters. "What happens if you get lost in there?"

"Each of the scarecrows has a pocket," answered Farmer Joe. "Inside the pocket you'll find specific directions to help you get back to the entrance."

"When can we have a look?" asked another reporter.

"How about now?" offered Farmer Joe. "Gather 'round, ladies and gentlemen. The Great Dalrymple Corn Maze is about to open!"

Chapter 5

Farmer Joe walked over to the maze's entrance just below the big banner. A scarecrow stood next to the entrance, holding an ENTER HERE sign. A yellow ribbon was attached to two cornstalks and hung across the entrance.

"Friends, it's my great pleasure to welcome you to the Great Dalrymple Corn Maze," proclaimed Farmer Joe. "I'm mighty proud of it and believe it will provide children and families with hours of pleasure. And now to assist me in the official opening, I'd like to invite up Miss Daphne Blake."

Daphne gasped in surprise. "Me?"

"Go on, Daph," Fred urged.

The rest of the gang clapped loudly as Daphne walked over to Farmer Joe. He picked a pair of giant hedge clippers up off the ground and handed them to her.

"Make sure you get a good shot of this," Farmer Joe reminded the photographers. "One . . . two . . ."

But before he could get to three, everyone heard a loud growl. Suddenly, the scarecrow holding the ENTER HERE sign sprang to life, tearing through the yellow ribbon.

"You fools!" he bellowed. "I warned you before to leave or pay the price. So now you will pay dearly. For every hour you remain, one of you will become my prisoner. I will not stop until this maze closes down forever!" Then the scarecrow grabbed Daphne. He threw her over his shoulder and disappeared into the maze.

The reporters were so stunned they didn't think to take pictures. Instead, they turned and ran for their cars.

"Wait! Where are you going?" Farmer Joe called.

"To get the story about the haunted farm to our newspapers!" one yelled back.

Meanwhile, Fred, Velma, Shaggy, and Scooby-Doo ran up to the maze's entrance.

"Come on, gang, we've got to find Daphne and the scarecrow," Fred said.

"Hold on there. That maze is so complex, they could be anywhere," Farmer Joe said. "You could spend hours in there and never find either of them."

"You've got a good point," Fred said. "Hmm. Could I see your plans for the maze, Farmer Joe?"

"Sure," Farmer Joe replied.

"Great," Fred said. "While I'm doing that, Velma, you, Shaggy, and Scooby can start searching for Daphne. Remember, if you get lost, check with the scarecrows."

"Sounds like a plan to me," Velma agreed. "Let's go, you two."

Fred and Farmer Joe headed back to the farmhouse. Velma, Shaggy, and Scooby walked into the maze and followed the path a short distance. As they did, Shaggy noticed something red hanging from a cornstalk. He reached over and picked up a red bandanna.

"Man, that Farmer Joe sure thought of everything," Shaggy said. "He even put out hankies so we could wipe our foreheads."

"That's no ordinary hanky, Shaggy," Velma said. "That's a clue. Daphne must have pulled it out of the scarecrow's pocket to tell us which way to go."

"Now that we know, what do you say we stop for a quick bite?" suggested Shaggy. "Hey, Scooby, do you want corn, corn, or corn?"

"Shaggy, this is no time for fooling around," scolded Velma. "Once we find Daphne and the scarecrow, I'll bet Farmer Joe will start the barbecue."

"Then what are we waiting for?" Shaggy exclaimed. "Come on, Scoob. To Daphne!"

"Roo Raphne!" Scooby echoed.

Chapter 6

Velma, Shaggy, and Scooby continued through the maze. They followed the path to the end, where they saw another scarecrow pointing in different directions.

"No clues from Daphne to help us this time," Velma said. "I think we'd better split up now. Shaggy and Scooby, you follow the path to the left. I'll go to the right. If you see anything, yell out my name. I'll find you by following your voice."

"Like, you got it, Velma," Shaggy said. "Let's go, Scoob. Maybe you can use that nose of yours to sniff out the way to Daphne."

Scooby put his nose to the ground and started sniffing around. He sniffed this way and that, but he couldn't find anything. Then a piece of hay tickled his nose.

"Ra-ra-ra-ra-ra-CHOOOOOOO!" sneezed Scooby. He did a test sniff with each nostril.

"Rahhhh, rat's retter," Scooby said. He put his nose back to the ground and started sniffing again. He quickly picked up a scent. He started walking so fast that Shaggy had to jog to keep up.

"Atta boy, Scoob," Shaggy said. "I knew you could do it. First we'll find Daphne, and then we'll find lunch!"

Scooby suddenly stopped in the middle of the path.

"What is it, Scoob?" asked Shaggy. "Is she here?"

Scooby sniffed around in the air. He sniffed at the cornstalks on the right side of the path, and then on the left side of the path.

"Rorry," Scooby said, shrugging his shoulders.

"At least you gave it a good try, Scoob," Shaggy said. "Now how do we get back to the entrance so we can find Velma?"

"Ri ron't row," Scooby said.

"You mean you don't remember the way out?" Shaggy asked. "Can't you, like, follow the smells in reverse?"

Before Scooby could answer, they both heard a rustling sound from the cornstalks.

"Did you hear that, Scoob?" asked Shaggy.

"Rup," Scooby said softly.

"Like, what are the chances it's Matilda the sheep?" Shaggy said.

The rustling got closer.

"Let's tiptoe out of here, Scoob," Shaggy whispered. They started tiptoeing backward down the path, watching the cornstalks for any sudden movements.

After a few yards, Shaggy bumped into something. He and Scooby froze. Shaggy looked down between his legs and saw the legs of a scarecrow standing behind him.

"Zoinks!" he gasped. "Scarecrow! Let's get out of here, Scooby-Doo!"

Shaggy and Scooby started running. The scarecrow followed close behind. "Help! Velma! Fred! Daphne! Anyone! Help!" Shaggy called as they raced away.

Chapter 7

The scarecrow chased Shaggy and Scooby up one path and down another. They ran through a series of twists and turns in the maze. Shaggy looked back, and the scarecrow was gone.

"Okay, Scoob, we can stop running now," he said. "I think he's gone."

As the two of them stopped to catch their breath, they heard more rustling in the cornstalks.

"Oh, no, not again," Shaggy moaned. The rustling got very close. Before Shaggy and

Scooby could run away, someone burst through the cornstalks.

"Daphne!" Shaggy cried. "We thought you were the scarecrow coming back to chase us again."

"Reah!" shouted Scooby, giving her a big Scooby hug.

"Shhhh!" Daphne whispered, holding her finger up to her lips. She motioned for Shaggy and Scooby to follow her. A few steps down the path, she noticed a piece of paper on the ground. She picked it up and unfolded it.

"Outta sight!" she exclaimed. "The scarecrow must have dropped this when he was chasing you."

Looking down at the paper every so often, Daphne led Shaggy and Scooby through the maze. Soon, they found themselves back at the entrance.

"Like, you saved us, Daphne," Shaggy said.

"Ranks!" barked Scooby, giving Daphne a lick on the cheek.

"You're welcome, Scooby," Daphne replied, laughing. "Hey, where's Fred and Velma?"

"Fred went back to the farmhouse with Farmer Joe," Shaggy answered. "And we got separated from Velma in the maze. Zoinks! I hope the scarecrow didn't get her!"

"Don't worry, he didn't," said Velma, walking out of the maze. "I couldn't find any more clues, so I followed the directions in the scarecrows' pockets."

Then Fred came into the clearing from the farmhouse path.

"Daphne! Am I glad to see you!" Fred said. "Are you all right?"

"I'm fine. I managed to run away from the

scarecrow when he put me down to rest," she said. "Then after Shaggy and Scooby found me, we saw this clue." She showed the others the folded-up piece of paper.

"Hey, that looks like the picture the kooky artist showed us," Shaggy said. "But what are all those numbers along the bottom? 15L, 20R, 10R, 25L? What do they mean?"

"They mean that we're one step closer to solving this mystery," Fred said. "I just finished studying Farmer Joe's map of the maze. And I learned one very important thing."

"What's that, Fred?" asked Daphne.

"The maze has only one solution," Fred explained. "That means there's only one correct path from the entrance to the middle and back out again."

"So, like, all we have to do is lock the entrance and wait for the scarecrow to try to come back out, right?" asked Shaggy.

"Shaggy, you can't lock cornstalks," Velma said.

"Then what's that key for?" Shaggy asked. He pointed to a key on the ground next to the entrance. It lay right next to a piece of torn yellow ribbon.

Velma knelt down and picked up the key. She blew off the dirt and examined it closely.

"Shaggy, I think you just helped solve our mystery," Velma said. She handed the key to Fred.

"Velma's right," Fred agreed. "And if that piece of paper means what I think it means, we don't have much time. So listen up, gang, it's time to set a trap."

Chapter 8

"**S**ooner or later, the scarecrow is going to come out of the maze," Fred began. "Our job is to get him to come out sooner."

"And how are we going to do that?" asked Shaggy. "Or don't I want to know?"

"We'll pretend that more visitors have arrived, and that they're going to take a hayride," Fred continued.

"Sorry, Fred, but I don't think the scarecrow is going to be in any mood for a hayride," Shaggy interrupted.

"No, but he'll be in the mood to scare the riders," Velma said.

"Right, and that's where you and Scooby come in," Fred said. "When the scarecrow comes out of the maze, Scooby, get him to chase you over to the hayride wagon. Shaggy and I will be there waiting. When the scarecrow shows up, we'll take him by surprise and throw one of those big burlap sacks over him."

"Congratulations, Fred old boy," Shaggy said, slapping Fred on the back. "You've done it again."

"Done what?" asked Fred.

"Come up with another plan that Scooby and I want nothing to do with," Shaggy answered.

"Is that true, Scooby?" asked Daphne.

Scooby thought for a moment, then he nodded.

"Reah," he said. "Rit's rue."

"That's too bad," Daphne said, shaking her head. "Because in addition to the big barbecue, I was going to offer you a Scooby Snack for helping us. But if you're not interested . . ."

"Rait!" Scooby barked. "Ri'll roo rit."

"Thanks, Scoob," Daphne said. "You're the bravest dog around!" She took a Scooby Snack from the box and tossed it into the air.

Scooby waited until just before it hit the ground before he lunged forward and caught it on his tongue.

"Nice move, Scooby," Shaggy said admiringly.

"Rank rou," Scooby replied.

"Enough kidding around," Fred said. "We'd better get a move on."

"I'll talk to Farmer Joe about helping us," Daphne said.

"And I'll go get a burlap sack from behind the farmhouse," Velma said. "I'll meet you by the hayride wagon."

The two girls ran down the path leading back to the farmhouse.

"Since there's only one way out of the maze, Scooby, you wait for the scarecrow here," Fred said. "When he comes out, get him to chase you down the farmhouse path. Run over to the hayride wagon, and we'll do the rest."

"Rokay," Scooby barked.

Fred and Shaggy walked down the path to get into their places. A moment later, Scooby heard Farmer Joe's voice over the loudspeaker.

"Welcome, newcomers," he said. "Welcome to Dalrymple Farm. Before we open the maze, please join us behind the farmhouse for a good old-fashioned hayride."

Scooby sat in front of the maze, waiting

for the scarecrow. He soon heard the familiar rustling of the cornstalks that meant someone was near.

"Ruh-roh," Scooby said aloud. At that moment, the scarecrow burst right through the middle of a row of cornstalks and ran straight at Scooby-Doo.

"Rikes!" barked Scooby. He scrambled to his feet and ran down the path back to the farmhouse. When he came out the other end, Scooby turned left and ran toward the

hayride wagon. The scarecrow wasn't far behind.

Shaggy was sitting on the tractor, wearing
a straw hat. "Over here, Scoob!" he called.
"I've got the engine on and everything."

Scooby jumped into the wagon. Before
the scarecrow could follow, Fred popped up
and tossed the burlap bag over his head. But
the scarecrow didn't let that stop him. He
ripped the bag open and jumped onto the
wagon. Then he pushed Fred off and turned
to Scooby-Doo.

Shaggy was so scared he jumped up and
released the brake by accident. The tractor
lurched forward, and Shaggy tumbled off.
The scarecrow was about to lunge for him, so
Scooby grabbed a pawful of hay and threw it
into the scarecrow's face. Then Scooby
jumped from the wagon into the driver's seat
of the tractor.

The tractor was still moving, so Scooby

started steering it all over the farm, trying to make the scarecrow lose his balance and fall off. Instead, the scarecrow reached down and unhooked the wagon from the tractor. Just as the wagon fell away, the scarecrow jumped onto the back of the tractor. He reached for Scooby. Scooby ducked away, losing control of the wheel.

The next thing Scooby knew, the tractor had plowed right into an enormous haystack.

The scarecrow got knocked off and landed on the ground with a thud. Fred ran over and grabbed a rope from the animal pen. He and Shaggy tied up the scarecrow as Farmer Joe, Velma, and Daphne came running over.

Chapter 9

"Is everyone all right?" asked Farmer Joe. "I think so," Fred said. "Now let's see who's really inside this scarecrow costume."

Farmer Joe reached over and yanked off the scarecrow's mask.

"Dusty!" Farmer Joe exclaimed. "It was you all along? I don't believe it."

"It's true, Farmer Joe," Velma said. "And it's just as we suspected."

"But how did you know?" asked the farmer.

"We didn't at first," Velma continued. "We

weren't sure of anything until we started finding clues."

"Like the red bandanna," Daphne said. "Dusty, Sally Ann, and Fortunato all had red bandannas when we met them. So when we found the bandanna inside the maze, that meant the scarecrow could be any one of them."

"But then Daphne found the second clue," Fred added. "It was this piece of paper." He showed it to Farmer Joe.

"Fifteen L, twenty R . . . Why, these look like directions," Farmer Joe said. "Fifteen steps to the left, twenty steps to the right."

"Exactly," Velma said. "But not just any directions. Directions to the maze. This sheet guided the scarecrow so he wouldn't get lost."

"And if the scarecrow needed directions,

then it couldn't have been Fortunato," Daphne said. "After all, he still had a copy of the maze that he showed Shaggy and Scooby. And since he designed the maze, he wouldn't need directions to help him get through it."

"So that left Sally Ann and Dusty," Velma said. "Both of them made it clear they wanted the maze to fail. But only one of them had access to the key."

"What key?" asked Farmer Joe.

"The key we found just outside the maze's entrance," Fred said, holding it up. "And it's the key — if I'm not mistaken — that unlocks the animal pen."

"Remember how Dusty said he saw the scarecrow open the pen and let the animals out?" Velma asked.

"Sure, and then he said

the scarecrow ran off into the cornfield," Farmer Joe recalled. "What about it?"

"None of it happened that way," Fred stated. "Dusty opened the gate himself and chased the animals out. He made up the whole thing."

"How do you know?" asked Farmer Joe.

"Because when he was complaining about the scare-crow, he mentioned the fact that the scare-crow was scaring visitors as they drove up," Daphne pointed out. "That was something we only told you, Farmer Joe. Dusty couldn't have known about that unless he was the scarecrow."

"Is all this true, Dusty?" asked Farmer Joe.

"Yes, okay?" Dusty replied angrily. "It's all true. I warned you not to mess around with the farm. I've been here thirty years, and I didn't want to see all my hard work get turned into a playground for city folks. So I was going to force you to close the maze and go back to farming. Just the crops, the animals, and me. And it was all going according to plan until those meddling kids and their nosy dog got in the way."

"Speaking of your nosy dog, where is he?" asked Farmer Joe.

"Omigosh!" Shaggy cried. "I forgot all about him." He rushed over to the haystack where the tractor had crashed and started looking through the hay.

"Scooby? Scooby-Doo, where are you?"

"Ra-ra-ra-ra-CHOOOOOOOOO!" Scooby sneezed from inside the haystack. A tuft of hay blew up into the air and Scooby's paw poked out. Shaggy reached over and gave him a big pull. Scooby-Doo came flying out of the haystack.

"Like, look at me," Shaggy said with a smile. "I just found a Scooby in a haystack!"

Everyone started laughing.

"Scooby-Dooby-ra-CHOOOO!" sneezed Scooby.

About the Author

As a boy, James Gelsey used to run home from school to watch the Scooby-Doo cartoons on television (only after finishing his homework). Today, he still enjoys watching them with his wife and two daughters. He also has a real dog named Scooby who loves nothing more than a good Scooby Snack!